HALFWAY HELL
PRODUCTIONS

PRESENTS

HELL MARY

Books I and II
Copyright: Drayton Wesley Jones, 2018

Written and Illustrated by Drayton W. Jones
Instagram @halfwayhell.productions

Cover Design by Hayley Selinski
Instagram @allhayldesigns

This series is dedicated to three important people. First, to my mom and my sister who show me superior examples of strong womanhood. Then, to my step-dad, who is the hardest worker I know. He always tells me to never go looking for a fight, but to always be ready for one. Family was the first institution. This story is for everyone who loves and fights for family.

THE WORLD FELL BECAUSE THE WORLD IS FALLEN, AND WHAT IS FALLEN, IS HELL. NOT FAR ENOUGH INTO THE FUTURE, THE WORLD IS NEARING DEATH. PRIMITIVE MEASURES OF SURVIVAL ARE NOW PRIORITIZED. MARY SOJOURNS HERE ON THIS DYING EARTH, PRAYING AND STRIVING TO SURVIVE JUST LONG ENOUGH. THIS IS HELL MARY, FULL OF WRATH, THE LORD IS WITH HER. LETHAL IS SHE AMONG WOMEN AND MEN. SHE SAVES SOME NOW, AND SOME AT THE HOUR OF THEIR DEATH. AMEN.

NIRVANA
hell Mary
DRAYTON JONES 18

BOOK I

I

Somewhere a white dove sat on a tree branch, covered in sunlight. Not in Hell. The sky was a deep purple there. It spread across the white brick city on the hill. No building was much taller than any other. Dried palm tree trunks lightly bent against the gusts of wind coming up from the dark sands. The sun said it's last goodbyes for the day and slipped beneath the horizon as the now dark sky blended with the ever-dark earth. Mary shifted slightly on her stomach causing a thud as the metal roof of the car popped up. She was small, barely 5'4", lean, with chopped dark haired. Her eyes were large and full of green. She had ten ear piercings in total and tattoos marked her dark tan skin on her right cheek and left arm. She wore green army pants, boots, and an old Nirvana t-shirt. Mary lay on top of a white 1957 Ford Fairlane with a 352 Thunderbird V8 engine. Tire chains covered all four tires and each were rusted in place. The wind pushed her short hair over the top of her head and down the left side of her face. She peered through the red dot sights on her M4. The large two storied building looked clear. *No Pirates, Darkfaces, or Crazies,* she thought.

Her head lifted as she lay her rifle next to her and pushed up with her arms to sit on the car roof. Six barked twice from the passenger seat beneath her, sticking his brown and black haired head out of the side window.

"Hush Six!" Mary whispered. The dog obeyed and pulled his head back into the car. Mary reached into her left cargo pocket and pulled out a crumpled pack of Camel's with one left. She retrieved a lighter from a small bag at her side. "Ya know Six, this is the last smoke I got but it doesn't matter. Can't smoke anymore after tonight anyway right?" Six yawned with a sigh and stuck out his tongue, panting.

The moon was full and reflected off of every white brick building and cracked up road. Sand dunes had formed on some of the open streets. Dried strands of brown grass snapped and waved in the wind as each stood momentarily in cracks in the road before being snipped off and carried away with each new gust. Mary and her car remained in darkness, parked at the very edge of the city, where the buildings stop and the dark sand begins; the edge of Hell. She finished her cigarette, flicked it into the sand, and jumped off the roof of the car, slinging her rifle over her shoulder. After a soft whistle, Six jumped out of the passenger window and followed her into the city.

Mary walked slowly as she approached a wide street with the two-story

building. She puller her rifle off of her shoulder and gripped the hand and fore grips positioning her finger a twitch away from the trigger. Her left hand released the grip

for a moment to motion for Six to sit at the entrance of the building, which was

covered by two rot-iron gates chained at the center. The left gate's bottom hinge

had rusted off and allowed the gate to be pulled forward from the bottom. Mary did

so and crawled through the open space on the other side. Six tilted his head as he

stared through the iron bars at his master. He stuck out his tongue and panted softly.

Mary put her left finger up to her lips and Six sat by the gate obediently. Alone she

stood in a marble courtyard. Much of the marble was cracked and there were

several rows of large columns holding up a now caved in roof. On the opposite wall

was a mural of some now forgotten war lord peppered with many bullet holes.

Lived in Havana my whole life and not once have I been in here, Mary thought.

A sign hung above a large door across the courtyard which read *Abortion*

and Insemination Clinic. Mary shuddered and then inhaled deeply as she walked

towards the door then, thrusting her leg forward, she kicked it open; she splintered

the wood at the hinges. Through the new opening was a dark hallway, illuminated

only momentarily by the flickering florescent lights which dangled by tangles of

cords from the ceiling. A slight buzz from the flickering lights masked all the other

sounds that could be in the hall. Mary tread slowly, rifle in hand, casting a dark

flickering silhouette against the cream colored walls. Flashes of smeared blood,

forceps, brass shells, and what looked like skin appeared on the floor with each

spasm of light that was briefly cast down. A crumpled and half rolled up poster lay

on the floor among the abandoned metal instruments and bits of human—infant and adult. Mary stepped on the bottom corner of the poster and pressed her other boot near the rolled half, sliding her foot up until the poster was flat. She flicked on the small light that was fastened next to the rifle's barrel. Printed on the poster were the words:

Free abortions up through the 40th week of Pregnancy.

Mary sighed and brushed the poster to the side with her foot. The hallway ended with an open doorway. Mary raised her rifle to guide the light into the pitch black; it was a windowless concrete room. Rows of metal shelving stood lined in rows, each containing what appeared to be glass tubes of red liquid. Her heart throbbed. She instinctively reached for her cargo pocket for a cigarette. *That's right, I just quit.* Her trigger finger quivered as it pointed straight forward. Her eyes tightened shut, then released open. A bead of sweat ran down her curved cheek and collected on her lips. She licked it before it fell to the floor. Mary rushed toward the third row. Each tube was labeled alphabetically; she knew where to go. *Castile.* The glass tube felt cold in her hand. Frantically she turned and strode over to a set of drawers and tore them open. One slid off of its rails and onto the floor, bursting apart. Syringes rolled a thousand directions across the dark cold floor. Mary grabbed the first one her fingers touched and slid the glass tube into the top opening. She pulled a needle out from her shirt and fastened it to the end of the syringe. Popping the light off of her rifle, she held it in her mouth as she peered down and lifted her shirt. *I have to do this now.* She thrust the needle into her lower abdomen and syringed the red liquid until the tube was empty.

"FUCK!" The light fell from her mouth as Mary pulled the needle out and dropped the tube onto the floor. She inhaled deeply several times and wiped sweat off of her face. Mary turned her head suddenly toward the doorway as she heard Six howl. Six only howls at two things. Other dogs…and Darkfaces. Mary gripped her rifle and fastened the light back into place as she sprinted out of the room and down the flickering hall, jumping over the pieces of wood from the kicked in door. She abruptly stopped once she stepped back out into the cool night of the courtyard. A soft blue glow was held by the marble as the moon peeked through the clouds.

"**Why are you in our city**?" a muffled robotic-like voice spoke but Mary could not see it's owner. She did not respond, but pulled her rifle up to her shoulder, peering through the sights. "**Havana is a dark zone**." There was still no sign of the disfigured voice's owner, or if it was alone.

"Six," Mary whispered. "**We have your dog**." Five tall figures dressed in black leather stepped out from behind several of the pillars. Each of their faces were covered in a sort of black material. Each wielded an AK-47 with a bayonet. "**Did you take some of the children?**" the one in the middle of the group spoke as he stepped forward. He slung his rifle over his shoulder and pointed at the kicked in doorway behind Mary, cocking his head to the side. "**Those children are to be raised as slaves. We will use them to save the world. You are a thief and a trespasser; you will come with us. Drop your weapon, NOW**."

"Hey fuck face, CATCH!" Mary threw her rifle at the dark figure in the center of the group and reached behind her, pulling out a Glock 17 from her back holster. ***CRACK! CRACK!*** Mary fired two shots at the two men to the left of the leader, snapping each of their heads back as the lead cut through their faces. Red splattered on the columns behind them. Mary dove behind a marble pillar. The two to the right of the leader raised their rifles and squeezed their triggers in unison, zipping .30 caliber bullets through the night, shattering bits and chunks of marble. The firing stopped and the sound of metal clinking across the ground grew closer as Mary saw a grenade roll past the column where she took refuge. She sprang up and leapt away as the explosion shot her even further through the air. Marble dust and bits rained down into the rubble of the courtyard. The three men shouted at each other. Mary's head felt heavy. Her vision blurred. She could barely make out the three silhouettes in the smoke. Suddenly, three flashes of light shot through the dust with a booming noise and each silhouette dropped with a thud to the marble floor. A new figure emerged from the dust. A tall man in boots, cargo pants and a tattered Levis jacket bent down, and holstered his Desert Eagle. His thick, rough hands gently lifted Mary's head and just before everything went black she heard him say, "My name is Jim, I'm going to help you, we have to leave now." *A saint*, she thought.

<u>II</u>

The Ford Fairlane crept slowly across the sand as it approached a large cage-like structure of bones and what looked like wax boulders at the base. Each bone was nearly twenty feet in height stretching up to the midnight blue sky littered with stars before curving at the ends back toward each other. The wind swept across the dunes of the dark sand with a slight howl, making it and the sound of the V8 engine the only audible noise in Hell.

Mary felt something warm, coarse, and wet rub across her cheek and up over her eye. She felt it again. Mary peeled her eyes open and sat up quickly. Six barked suddenly and panted, half climbing into her lap. Mary swiveled her head around sharply looking for her gun. Jim caught her eyes in the rearview mirror.

"Good, you're awake," he almost whispered. Mary saw her M4 propped up in the front seat. She shot her arm forward, grasping the fore grip. "Easy," Jim said coolly. He had already un-holstered his pistol and had the barrel pointed at her temple. "I'm gonna pull over here and then you can drive when I'm sure your head's good, alright?" Jim holstered his gun and quickly pressed on the brakes and shut off the ignition. Opening the driver's door Jim stood and walked over toward one of the large bones and propped against it with one hand and rested the other on his hip. Mary noticed red splatters across his jean jacket and his hands. Six crawled his front half across Mary and poked his head out of the window and waged his tail.

———

13

"You like him, huh?" Mary whispered in his ear and she pet his neck with both of her hands. "We'll see." She opened the door to let Six jump out and then retrieved the keys and her rifle before slowly walking over to Jim.

"So I guess you saved us huh?"

"Right place, right time I guess." Jim turned around and reached into his front jacket pocket for a cigarette. He raised his eyebrows toward Mary.

"I quit." she shook her head as she spoke. Jim shrugged his shoulders and retrieved his lighter.

"So why were you in Havana?" she asked.

"Real question is why were *you*?" Jim spoke as his cigarette bobbed up and down between his lips. He drew in a long drag and blew out the white smoke into the night air. You have a nice car. V8. Full tank, two weapons, a good dog," Six kept wagging his tail as he stood by Mary. "And a million reasons I'm sure to be nowhere near hell."

"There was something there I needed."

"That bad? "

"Yes. Something I can't live without."

"Well…" Jim paused and lifted his eyebrows again toward Mary.

"My name is Mary."

"Well Mary. We should camp out here. It's relatively safe. Haven't seen any Crazies for three weeks. Only a few Pirate ships here and there. We'll build a small fire, cook some dinner, and then you can tell me what it is you can't live without."

Six panted and barked with approval, nudging Mary in the hip with his head. She nodded.

"Ok. But I don't remember your name."

"Me neither." Jim said casually as he walked past Mary towards the car. He turned and pulled his jacket back on the right side and pointed to a patch sewn onto a mechanic's shirt.

"Jim." Mary said.

"First shirt I found after I escaped. Didn't remember my name, so I thought this was as good as any." Mary grinned.

"I hope you don't mind; I threw my bag in your trunk." Jim held out his hand. "Keys?"

III

A single cloud drifted across the dark sky temporarily hiding the moon from view. The other light came from the thousands of stars and the small fire below. Jim had begun to cook a small pot of beans over the fire as he had suggested and Six had turned around three times in the sand and then lay down, content in his new bed. Mary leaned against the driver's door of her car as she checked her rifle's chamber and barrel for sand. Jim crouched down and dug in his bag, pulling out two small bowls.

"Where did you find an M4?" Jim raised his eyebrows as he dipped each bowl into the simmering pot.

"Guantanamo Bay." Mary grinned.

"No shit? Well that's as good a place as any." Jim handed a bowl to Mary. "Sorry, no spoons." Six cocked his head to the side as he watched the food passed across the fire. "Right, almost forgot." Jim reached in his bag and pulled out an unusually large bone and tossed it to Six. He caught it in his mouth and immediately began wagging his tail as he chewed on one of the ends. Mary's eyes pleaded for an explanation. "Tiger bone. It escaped from a zoo…" Her eyes widened. "It's a long story." Jim then reached inside his jacket. Mary instinctively released the bolt catch on her M4 and flipped the fire selector to auto with her thumb and lined the sights at Jim's head. Six reared up and barked. Jim

---

16

immediately threw his hands up, dropping his bowl. "Holy Shit!"

"What were you reaching for?!" Mary maintained her aim.

"What?"

"Why did you reach into your jacket?" Mary's lips moved forcefully.

"I found some rum a few days back. Was gonna take a sip—look, you need to calm down."

"There is no calm—we're in Hell, remember."

"I'm sorry, you're right." Jim sighed. "Okay? *You're right.*" Jim said softly.

Mary slowly lowered her rifle.

"Look, you want some rum?" Jim grinned. She sat her rifle down in her lap and picked up her bowl.

"Sorry I made you drop your food. And no, I can't drink."

"What, are you knocked up or something?" Jim laughed as he talked. Mary just stared at him across the fire.

"Oh. Son of a bitch. You're pregnant."

"That's why I was in the clinic. In Havana. My dead husband's DNA was there. We promised we would have a family right before…before the world died. I promised. That's what I can't live without. *Our child.*" Mary spoke slowly and calmly. Jim stared at the fire before taking a slow sip of rum and then tossing the bottle over toward his bag.

"Look. I think you're fucking crazy." Jim rolled his eyes at himself as Mary shot him a look. "What I mean is…look, crazy was the wrong word." He quickly broke eye contact and stared at his spilt bowl of beans that has soaked into the dark sand.

"You're the crazy one." Mary grinned, stretching out her leg and poking Jim's boot with the tow of her boot. "Calling a pregnant woman *crazy*… that's playing with some fucking fire ya think?" He looked up, smiled, and then burst out a quick explosion of laughter. Six perked his head up, giving the large bone a quick respite.

"So where you headed?" Jim said, fighting laughter.

"Badlands." Mary replied quickly.

"Badlands? Like, the old Dakota states Badlands?! Holy shit. *Ho-ly Shit!*" Jim shook his head.

"It's nearly 3,000 miles away." Mary turned her head towards Six who stuck out his tongue and panted. "Holy Shit."

"Why? What's there?" Jim stared intently at her eyes.

"It's where my husband was from. He had said it was one of the few places in the world that hadn't fully died yet. There are still wild flowers. There are no rapists, or pirates, or gangs. Just people. Maybe even good ones."

"It sounds great." Jim sighed. "But I'll believe it when I see it."

"You think it isn't real?" Mary asked straightly.

"I don't know many things that are real anymore."

"What do you know?"

"I know that if you bleed enough, you die." Jim stared once more at the fire.

It was starting to die. Mary reached over to pet Six's neck, but kept staring at Jim. His eyes glossed a bit.

"Well," Mary said, trying to sound cheerful, "do you know what the fuck this thing is here in the middle of Hell?" She nodded to the large pillars and wax like boulders behind Jim.

"Of course." Jim said, sitting up. "It's a whale carcass." Mary gasped a little.

"I didn't know any remains of the before-creatures were left."

"Most are gone. I've seen some before-creatures near the Mexican cliffs. I think the Dark-Face Lord keeps them as pets." Jim sighed. "Well, since you made me spill my food…"

"Yeah, sorry about that." Mary frowned.

"It's fine, but I'm gonna go see if I can scavenge something. I found an abandoned truck the other day. Maybe 3 miles west of here." The moment Jim stopped speaking, they heard a shrill scream, eerily close. Jim sprang up, unholstering one of his Desert Eagles. Mary flicked her safety selector to full auto as she vaulted to her feet.

"It seems to be just on the other side of the whale," she whispered.

"Ok." Jim said as he began motioning with his free hand. "I'll go around the tail, you advance up and come around the head. Hopefully there's no more than two."

"Two what?"

"Crazies."

Mary nodded and watched Jim disappear around the back side of the carcass. She turned and signaled for Six to follow at her side. Creeping towards the head of the whale, she pointed her rifle directly forward. ***CRACK! CRACK!*** Mary knew that sound. Desert Eagles made a distinct thud when they were fired. She turned and saw dull light flash twice through the rotting fat of the whale. "Six!" Mary whispered and motioned him to begin running with her. Mary reached the head of the whale and turned the corner. She almost yelled for Jim when something slammed into her stomach. She heard a small voice gasp. Mary fell and rolled over in the sand, facing a young, wide eyed girl with bright red hair. She couldn't have been more than twelve years old.

"Mary!" Jim yelled as he sprinted towards them. Suddenly, a mound of sand began to shift and pour off of a dark rising figure. As the sand fell, suddenly a large man stood just feet from Mary and the young girl, covered in black robes and a red cloth mask. He raised an AK-47 at the girl. Mary whistled for Six who grabbed the girl's collar in his mouth and began to drag her away.

CRACKKKKKCRACKKK!! The dark figure missed his first several shots at the girl's head. Mary rolled to grab her rifle and fired two quick shots at the figure's knees. A fierce cracking noise was made when the 5.56 rounds ripped through his flesh and bone. He dropped to his knees and screamed. Mary recovered her aim and aligned the sights on his face.

"Wait!" Jim gasped as he caught his breath. We need the ammo." Mary slowly lowered her rifle and Jim flicked a karambit knife from his belt and sunk the blade into the man's throat, running it across from one side to the other. Red seeped through the fabric and splattered onto the sand as the man in black collapsed forward onto the ground. "Fuckin' crazies."

"You ok?" Mary asked.

"Never been better. Where's the girl?"

"Shit! Six! Come Six!" Mary shot up and the two ran back towards the car. They darted around the side of the whale and nearly ran into Six who barked twice the moment he saw Mary. Mary furrowed her brow. They heard the sound of an engine starting and tires spinning in the sand. The Ford Fairlane sped off into the distance.

"She stole my car!" Mary exclaimed.

"Well shit. She stole your car." Jim said, taking out another cigarette.

<u>IV</u>

Mary and Jim left dark footprints in the dark sand as they walked back toward Havana. Six stayed several yards out in front, sniffing the ground. Each grain of sand shimmered a little as it was overturn by their boots and briefly caught the light of the moon. Mary carried her M4 and Jim had taken the AK from the dead crazy.

"Do you think it was a setup?" Mary asked.

"I think she was just scared." Jim's cigarette bobbed up and down as he spoke. "Crazies don't keep children. They kill them, or worse. She was probably just trying to escape."

"How many hours of darkness do we have left?"

"Hmm." Jim looked up at the sky. "Maybe four."

"We can't be caught out here in the light. It exposes all of Hell. That's how people get caught." Mary sighed. A soft rumbling grew into a prominent noise.

"I know that sound." Jim suddenly stopped.

"It's a pirate ship!" Mary whispered. Jim nodded toward a small dune to their left. Six turned his head back to them and barked at Mary. The two sprinted across the sand as Six followed. Two lights shone against another sand dune further ahead and then turned to face them. The diesel engine grew louder. They sprinted

—

23

faster, kicking up sand with furious steps. Suddenly Jim's feet sank and he disappeared into a hole.

"Jim!" Mary turned and saw the sand begin to disappear in front of her and she jumped to the side before the ground gave way. Six whimpered as he carefully stepped towards the edge of the hole and cocked his head to the side, looking down at Jim.

"I'm ok!" Jim coughed in the darkness. "I've seen these before. They're…"

"Slave-traps." Mary whispered to herself, staring at the tattoo on her arm. The diesel ship was upon them now. Mary looked up from the pit and stared straight ahead past the bright lights. Her and Six's silhouettes stood tall and black against the blinding brightness of the truck. It stopped just before the pit making a sharp high pitched noise as it braked. The ship was a large black semi-truck with tank treads where the wheels would normally be. It pulled a black yacht on a trailer with a large black flag. Seven men poured out of the truck and the boat. All were armed with M4s, Glocks, and AKs. They had boots and military pants and jackets. The two men in front, the apparent leaders, wore navy berets.

"Welllll Shit." The first man with the beret said as he shone his Glock with a mounted light into the pit. He had a thick beard and a scar over his left eye. "The female is the one that's supposed to fall in the trap, not this piece of …" The man studied Jim's face, "Tex-Mex trash." He spat into the pit as Jim stepped out of the way. The man glanced up as he wiped his beard. "Drop that M4 right now sweetie before I kill Tex here." Mary glanced down at Jim who shook his head. She tossed the rifle to the ground. "Now tell me something sweetie. You face fuck?" The other men began to laugh and grin. "Cause they pay extra for face fuckin." Mary reached behind for her 6o'clock holster and pulled out her Glock 17. ***CRACK! CRACK!*** She hit the man in the face and the neck. Blood splattered on the men directly behind him and gushed from the left artery in his neck as he fell forward into the pit.

"You mean like that?" Mary said, taking aim at the other leader. Clicking noises mixed with shouts were heard as the other men moved their safety selectors to full auto and aimed at Mary's head. One of the grunts strode forward and grabbed what looked like a small crossbow that had been slung on his waist and shot it at Mary. The arrow nicked her shoulder and pierced her shirt, hooking onto the collar. The arrowhead was fastened to a wire and was suddenly yanked back by the man, ripping the shirt from her. The men resumed their laugher. Six jumped in front of Mary and growled at them, barring his teeth.

"That's called a no means yes hook" The grunt said laughing as he pulled the shirt back to him. As he reeled in the wire, it fell into the pit and stopped. He tugged on the wire twice. "Fuckin' piece of…" Suddenly the man disappeared into the pit as the wire pulled him in. **_CRACK!_** Bits of brain, bone, bloody hair, and flesh shot up out of the pit.

"ENOUGH!" Exclaimed the other pirate with the beret. He reached for a flash grenade on his belt, pulled the pin, and dropped it into the pit.

"Jim!" Mary screamed as she saw him cover himself with the half-headed grunt. Desert Eagle rounds will do that to a head. The leader then shot a Taser at Mary who collapsed onto the ground. Everything went dark as Six lay beside her.

Mary jolted forward. She was still shirtless, wearing a black bra and her camo pants. Her boots and socks had been taken. Her eyes focused and she quickly grabbed a blanket that she just noticed and draped it over herself. Seven other girls were in the room sitting against the opposite wall. Seven. The youngest looked about 13, while the oldest appeared around Mary's age. Some wore dirty old jumpsuits while others were simply in pants and bras as Mary was. The room was lit by a single bulb. It was dark and green and rusted.

"Where are we?" Mary asked hoarsely. Her mouth was very dry.

"The hull of the ship. Harrod's ship." Said the oldest. She had black hair and was wearing one of the dirty jumpsuits. She was pregnant.

"Who the fuck is Harrod?" Mary said as she spat out some dried blood.

"He's one of Captain Hyde's pirates. Capt. Hyde of the Blackship Pirates. Harrod, He…" She stopped speaking and took a few steps forward towards Mary and began to whisper. "He sells sex slaves to the Blackfaces and the Crazies."

"How do you know this?"

"I'm Harrod's wife. Elizabeth." KNOCK! KNOCK! Mary startled back from the door. It creaked open. The man in the navy beret stepped in. He had a dark goatee and wore sunglasses. *It's fuckin' dark in here*, thought Mary.

"You're turn," he said, looking at Mary.

Jim thrust himself forward, sitting up aggressively, nostrils flaring as he inhaled.

"Calm down son, calm down!" An elderly man who had been sitting on the floor against the wall slowly stood. He had a large stick which worked as his cane. He was severely bent over, and looked nearly eighty. He wore a single grey robe. Jim was sitting on a thin blanket on a cold metal floor in a rusting metal room with a single light bulb dangling from a wire in the middle of the ceiling. Jim was shirtless and his boots had also been taken.

"Where is SHE?!" Jim snarled.

"Who? Who is she?" The old man's voice creaked as he spoke.

"We were captured by" Jim was interrupted by the old man's soft voice.

"Yes, yes, by the Blackship Pirates. Your friend was probably taken to…" The man paused.

"Where?!" Jim pleaded.

"Down the hall." The man frowned and turned to sit back down.

"What's down the hall?" Jim stood.

"Harrod's harem. He sells sex slaves. Mostly to the Blackfaces, sometimes to the Crazies if they are willing to negotiate—and that's a big if." Jim strode towards the metal door. It had a single wheel in the center of it, like a submarine. The wheel wouldn't budge. Jim prided himself on his strong hands. Mechanic's hands. "It's locked unless the guard opens it to bring food."

"What's your name? Why are you here?" Jim asked as he sighed and walked back over to the man. Jim leaned against the wall and slid down next to him.

"My name is Zachariah." The man spoke softly. His eyes glossed a little. "I was just a drifter, like you. Now I'm kept here to work, when I can. I'm a good cook."

"I thought the Blackships only dealt in arms and cocaine. Sex slaves too?" Jim stared at the door as he spoke. His large muscles moving up and down slowly with each heavy breath.

"They did. My guess is that this Harrod, the captain of this ship, began running girls on the side."

AHHHGH! A loud scream shot down the hallway from the other side of the door. Jim shot up to his feet. "That's Mary!" Jim's breath's quickened. He jumped towards the door and began banging on it with his fists. "Where did you say that room was?"

"Down the hall, to the right. Door at the very end."

"Good. When they come. When they open the door. Knock the light with your cane." Jim stared at the man who nodded reassuringly back at him.

"HEY!" yelled a voice from the other side of the door. "SHUT THE FUCK UP!"

"Come in here and MAKE ME!" Jim yelled back. The wheel on the door turned. Jim nodded toward Zachariah who shattered the light bulb with his cane. It was now pitch black. A thin stream of light appeared when the door opened. A large man in military gear stepped in. Jim saw the knife on his belt. By the time the man had stepped into the room Jim had jumped on the man's back with his left arm wrapped tightly around his neck. *UGH!* The man spun wildly and slammed Jim against the walls several times. Jim's lungs struggled. His breath was gone. He reached blindly for the man's knife. He found the handle, removed it from its sheath and stabbed the man in the stomach. Once. Twice. Threefourfivesixseveneight times. He did it so fast that the blood was delayed in spurting out. The man slowly dropped to his knees and Jim's feet now touched the floor as he stepped over the man's head, gripping his hair with his fist momentarily before shoving him down. Jim noticed the man's pistol and took it, shoving it into the waist of his pants. He stood momentarily in the doorway. A dark silhouette covered in blood, turning to the right.

<u>V</u>

"She was found driving a Ford Fairlane sir." A tall man with a moustache and a red beret had walked into a large cabin aboard the Black Phantom. The room had red carpet, with dark wooden walls and ceiling. It was dimly lit by Victorian style lamps on dark wood furniture. On the wall behind the Captain's desk was a large map of the Gulf of Mexico. Captain Hyde stood from his chair. His two Dalmatians stood as well. He was very large. Nearly 6'6", heavy, with a large grey beard. He wore a Navy jacket, cargo pants, and boots. His belt held a holstered Colt .45. He strode across the room. His two Dalmatians followed.

"Where is she?" His voice boomed.

"She is aboard Harrod's cruiser. He will be arriving here at the Phantom at 0500." The man stopped and sighed as if he were going to continue speaking.

"What is it Daniels?" Captain Hyde spoke firmly as he pet the top of one of the dog's heads. The other whimpered for attention. Hyde looked down at them. "Hush Nero! I am petting Marcus." He stepped closer to Daniels, inches from his face. "Just tell Harrod to *not* delay. I *MUST* see Elizabeth!"

Miles away, Harrod's cruiser sped along the dunes in the dark. The diesel engine hummed and the two bright headlights shone ahead, prompting sidewinders and rats to retreat to their holes and hideaways. *AGHH!* Jim sprinted down the dark green and brown rusted hallway as Mary's screams grew louder. His nostrils snarled. His teeth were clenched. His face set. He reached the cracked door at the end of the hall and kicked it open. Mary was handcuffed to a bed. There were five men in the room; Harrod stood behind the bed trying to restrain Mary's legs. One of the men kept trying to dodge Mary's kicks as he tried to pull off her pants; the other three men stood at attention by the door. Every head turned once the door swung open. Jim wasted no time pulling the pistol from his waistband and shooting the man in the head who had been struggling at Mary's legs. Two men at the door grabbed Jim's arms and knocked the gun from his hand. Harrod began to crawl over the bed when Mary kicked him in the chest. He turned and punched her in the throat; she wheezed and gasped.

Jim pushed against the floor and slammed the two men against the wall, knocking him loose from their grip. He leapt over towards Harrod who was just stepping off of the bed. Jim punched him in the face, knocking him back against the wall. Before Harrod could regain his balance Jim punched him in the face again. *"LET HER GO!"* Jim spat and nearly frothed at the mouth as he spoke. Harrod looked up at Jim, blood dripping from his nose and lip. He grinned.

"Jim! Look out!" Mary screamed.

Jim started to turn then suddenly shook violently as he was tasered to the floor. Three other men in dark military uniforms and AK-47s entered the room.

"Sir, we have arrived at the Phantom." Harrod slowly stood, wiping the blood from his lip.

"Bring them up to the deck." He spat on Mary and laughed, walking out of the room.

The Black Phantom was a large ship. Two dark green military trucks pulled an oversized trailer which held up a large black Navy cruiser. Captain Hyde stood on the deck by the wheel with two guards in red berets next to him. Twenty men lined the deck against the rails. It was nearly dawn. Pink and deep blue light lined the horizon. Harrod's cruiser pulled up next to the Phantom's deck. The heavy purr of the diesel engine shut off. Two thin, white haired men in grey jumpsuits lowered a metal bridge with chain railing for Harrod to cross. He gestured for his men to follow with Jim and Mary. One of the pirates squeezed Mary's ass as she stepped onto the bridge. Turning quickly, she kicked the man over the side of the rail and down into the sand. His neck had snapped; a permanent look of shock rested on his face as blood began to soak the sand.

"Contain the prisoners!" Harrod exclaimed, turning to his men and unholstering his pistol. He pointed it towards a frightened young pirate. "Understand?"

"Harrod, what prisoners are those?" Hyde shouted, his voice booming from the other ship.

"My Captain!" Harrod lifted his arms to Hyde as he turned and crossed the bridge. "I have saved your daughter Elizabeth from these drifters!"

"Harrod, my friend, bring her! Where is she?!"

"My men are retrieving her as we speak." Harrod turned back and glared at Jim, then grinned at Mary as he stared at her bra. "These two tried to buy Elizabeth from the Darkfaces."

"Bring them Immediately!" Captain Hyde's voice boomed. He gestured to his two lieutenants with his Colt .45. The two pirates dressed in navy camo jumped the railing on the deck and sprinted toward the the bridge and took Mary and Jim. Captain Hyde then motioned with his hand for his men to put them on their knees as he descended to the deck. The two pirates shoved them onto the deck floor and aimed their rifles at the back of their heads. Jim's head slammed against the hardwood first, but he extended his leg just in time to catch Mary's, breaking her fall. They both struggled to their knees. Hyde's black combat boots echoed across the deck as he walked towards them. "You," the Captain spoke aggressively towards Jim. "you tried to BUY my daughter?!" Captain Hyde jabbed Jim in the chest with the muzzle of his pistol. He raised the barrel, running it up Jim's chest and using it to pull up his jaw. Hyde knelt down and the two locked eyes. "Did you?"

"PA-PA!" A young girl, around twelve years old with bright red hair emerged from below deck aboard Harrods's ship. She began sprinting across the bridge. Harrod turned, wide eyed, glaring at his men. As she ran to her father she locked eyes with Mary and suddenly stopped.

"Elizabeth! Hyde exclaimed, wide-eyed. "Come! What is wrong? These people will not…"

"She saved me." The young girl then sprinted over towards Mary, embracing her neck. One of the pirates reached for the girl's arm.

"Stop!" Hyde barked at the lieutenant. "Elizabeth. Come." He stood and backed up from Jim, motioning for his daughter. "This woman saved you?" He pointed at Mary.

"Yes pa-pa. And the man. They killed two Crazies who had tried to rape me." Hyde's face grew pale. He shot a glance at Jim. Suddenly, the sound of a woman's scream sounded from Harrod's cruiser. Another pirate sprinted from below, almost tripping over some of the other men as he weaved his way to the bridge.

"Captain Hyde!" he exclaimed, his hands shook as he clutched his rifle. "Captain Hyde! Cecilia is below in the infirmary. The medic was trying… he was…." The pirate pointed at Harrod.

"Shut your face private, Captain Hyde is dealing with an important matter!" Harrod snapped at the shaking man.

"No," the private said quietly.

"Excuse me?!" Harrod strode over to the man and unholstered his pistol.

"Harrod, let the man speak." Hyde stood and gently pushed Elizabeth behind one of his men.

"Captain!" the man exclaimed. Harrod pressed the muzzle of his pistol into the man's chest.

"He is disobeying my order's Captain; we will deal with this later." Harrod sneered and turned toward Hyde.

"No, you are disobeying *MINE*. We will deal with all of this now." Hyde's voice thundered. Everyone on deck was silent.

"Harrod's wife was forced to have an abortion!" The private had mustered up just enough courage to yell every word. It was silent for several seconds after he spoke. Harrod clenched his teeth and turned back towards the man. Captain Hyde snapped his finger. In one swift motion, his two lieutenants cut through the rope which fettered Jim and Mary while two other pirates rushed to restrain Harrod.

"Children," the Captain began, "are the lifeblood of our existence. *You*, Harrod, lied about these drifters!" Hyde swiftly closed in towards Harrod as he spoke. "*You* tried to kill your wife's child! You endangered *MY DAUGHTER*!"

Harrod startled back, struggling against the men who restrained him. "I, she…"

"You know the penalty for lying; for murder!" Hyde exclaimed.

"I will not be exiled!" Harrod exclaimed. He then thrust his head forward, ramming one of the lieutenant's heads, knocking him unconscious. As the guard fell to the deck, Harrod grabbed his pistol and shot the other lieutenant in the face, then quickly turned, aiming at Hyde. He lined up the sights, pulling the trigger back. WHAM! Jim tackled Harrod, pinning him prone to the deck, digging his elbow into Harrod's head. The stray bullet zipped past Hyde.

"You're *DONE*!" Jim spat through clinched teeth.

"So you wanted to sell your own wife? And this man's *child*?" Mary stood up tall as spoke. Every man turned and was silent. The desert wind blew and caught Mary's hair. She strode slowly towards Harrod who struggled in vain against Jim's hold. "I risked everything to find my husband's DNA in an abandoned clinic, but I found it. I am now pregnant. You tried to abort your own child. You tried to have me raped and sold. You tried to have *her* raped and sold." Mary said, pointing to Elizabeth.

"Just…J-just let me go. I'll go and never come back!" Harrod struggled to speak as Jim pressed into his throat. "I g-get it. I'm exiled!"

"Exiled?" Captain Hyde stepped forward. "No! No, you'll be executed." Mary reached down for Harrod's black HK .45 which lay on the deck. Hyde nodded. Harrod struggled, looking up through the corner of his eye at her.

"So, you're gonna murder me, huh bitch?"

"No. This isn't murder. This is judgement. And *this* is mine now." Mary's lips moved firmly as she spoke, her thumb cocking the hammer and her finger pulling the trigger. ***CRACK!!*** Jim had tucked his head into his shoulder. Bits of flesh flew and dark blood pooled beneath Harrod's head, spreading across the hardwood. Jim shoved off of the lifeless chest as he stood. He looked at Mary. She stared at the pool of blood; it was dark like the sand.

VI

The sun began to creep over the dark pink and purple peaks of the sand dunes. Mary stood at the edge of the deck, wrapped in a blanket, with new tan boots covering her feet. Six lay next to Elizabeth a few feet away, licking her face as she giggled and hugged his neck. Captain Hyde smiled at his daughter. His eyes were relaxed now, soft, deep. He turned to Mary.

"I can't repay you." Hyde sighed.

"This is more than enough." Mary said, looking down at the black Land Rover parked on the sand.

"It's the least I could do," Hyde said. "You saved my Elizabeth. My life. Children are the future." Mary looked down and grinned.

"I know."

"There's plenty of water, whatever food we had to spare, and several AK-47s with 6 extra loaded mags. And you can keep that," Hyde nodded towards the pistol holstered at Mary's side. "The dead don't need it." Hyde turned as Jim approached, who had stopped briefly to rub Six's head.

"This is all I could find." Jim said, tossing Mary a black t-shirt.

"Metallica?" She looked up at him. "I do like the coiled snake." Jim turned as Mary dropped the blanket and slipped the black shirt on.

"Well, no one's gonna tread on you." Jim winked. "I know it's not Nirvana, but hey check out this Army jacket, it says Joseph!" Jim rolled his eyes.

"Well you'll always be Jim to me," Mary laughed. Captain Hyde walked over to his daughter ran his thick fingers through her red hair. Come on darling, time to say good bye. Elizabeth ran to Mary and hugged her waist, pressing her head into her stomach. Several tears formed in Mary's eyes as she embraced her. Each dripped down her cheek and fell into the girl's hair.

"Don't steal anymore cars, alright?" Jim grinned. Elizabeth let go of Mary and almost tackled Jim with her hug. "Hey! Alright, be good, kid." Elizabeth stepped back and blew Mary a kiss, who caught it and put it in her pocket. She took her father's hand and the two walked below deck.

"This should get us to the Badlands, right?" Mary asked.

"Should get us pretty far regardless." Jim nodded, looking down at their new ride.

"I'm glad you decided to come with me." Mary said.

"Well I didn't have anything better to do anyway." Jim grinned.

"And if anyone gets in our way, we'll fuck 'em up!"

"Hell, Mary!" Jim laughed. "Yeah, we will." Six jumped up and nudged Mary in the back of the knee. His dark brown hair and pointy ears rubbing against her pants.

"You too Six." Mary said rubbing his neck. She peered out at the dark sands. Still nearly black even in the light of the sun. She closed her eyes. A white dove rested on a large tree branch. A little boy played in a clear blue stream. Her eyes shot open. The sand was still black.

"You good?" Jim asked, nudging her arm.

"Yeah. Now let's blow this motherfucker."

Prayton Jones 2018

BOOK II

<u>I</u>

"Drop it motherfucker!" Mary spat from across the large room. She stood at the double-door entrance of the strip club *Shark Attack*, wearing a black leather jacket with the name 'MADONNA' across the back over a new Nirvana t-shirt. The room was dim, lit mostly by the pink and blue neon reflecting against the mirrors and silver poles. Purple leather couches were scattered across the old molding carpet. Base thumped through the speakers. Mary aligned the sights of her MPX on the head of the tall muscular man with a green mohawk on the opposite side of the room. He wore a leather vest, was bare-chested underneath, and covered in tattoos. He held a desert eagle to one of the stripper's head's as he tightened his other arm around her neck. Nearly fifteen other men stood behind him, each armed with an automatic weapon and equally covered in leather gear and tattoos. A few of the club's workers hid behind the entrance counter or back in the bathroom hallway.

"So you're the pussy who's gonna try to save *this* pussy, huh?" The man with the green mohawk sneered at Mary, aggressively waving his pistol from the girl, towards Mary, and back towards the girl. *Way to sweep half the room dipshit,* Mary thought. "Listen, I don't know what you think you are gonna do with that gun against all of us, all by yourself…" He paused a moment to lick his lips. "But I know what all of us can do with that ass you got." He grinned. The men behind him snickered and laughed. The stripper struggled in vain against his grip. Three of the men then strode back toward the restroom only to quickly drag three other strippers who screamed as they were pulled across the floor by their hair. Mary clenched her teeth and rested her finger on the trigger.

The man with the mohawk pressed the muzzle of the pistol into the woman's temple. "Last chance to surrender sweetie," he said. "You can't hit me from there."

"Maybe not," Mary sighed. "But *he* can."

From the back right corner of the room, three men shot through the swinging kitchen doors. Jim was one of them. ***Crackkkkcrackkcrackkk!***

Jim fired his AK-47 in bursts, dropping five of the men in the back of the group and hitting the man with the green mohawk in the hip, forcing him to release the woman. The other two men who were with Jim split directions; the dark haired man went behind the group and the blonde man cut up towards the front as Jim advanced down the middle of the tattooed men gang.

The tattooed men swung their weapons violently from aiming at Mary to aiming at Jim, each pulling their triggers. Mary grabbed the screaming woman by the arm and both dove behind one of the purple couches. The other three women broke free, diving behind another one just next to them. ***Crackkkcrakkkkk***

Crackkk!!!! The blonde man toward the front dropped his AK that was now empty and unholstered his Glock shooting one of the men in the throat who had dragged one of the women. "That's my wife!" he exclaimed as the bullet ripped through his throat and splattered the men behind him with blood. The dark haired man in the back pinned two men against the wall, aligning their tattooed heads as Jim pulled the trigger to his AK, cutting through them simultaneously with a single burst of fire.

Jim quickly turned and aimed at another man and pulled the trigger. "Fuck." Jim said, realizing his magazine was empty. He dropped the AK and pulled out a tomahawk from his belt. ***Shinnng!!*** He sliced the man's neck open, dropping him to his knees as blood pooled on the carpet. Then, in a continuous motion, Jim stabbed another man in the eye with the pick end. Three men remained and turned to fire at Jim. Mary sprang up and emptied her magazine into them as 9mm rounds ripped and shredded the men. The brass casings clinked to the ground before the streams of blood began to cascade. Jim looked back at her and grinned, covered in sweat and blood. He then nodded toward the other two men, who ran towards two of the women and embraced them, crying.

The man with the green mohawk began to crawl across the carpet towards the back of the room, holding his open, bleeding side together as best he could. Mary strode over as Jim handed her the desert eagle from the floor.

"Y-you b-bit-tch!" The man coughed blood as he spoke. ***Crack!!!*** Blood and flesh sprayed the carpet and walls after Mary pulled the trigger; .50 caliber rounds will do that to a person's head.

An elderly man stood up from behind the front counter with his hands up.

He wore a tattered short-sleeve shirt. He shivered.

"Do you realize what you've d-d-done?!" He exclaimed, almost whispering.

"This is Saint Mako's club…He w-won't like it."

"We know," Mary sighed. "We'll fuck him up too."

"What she said." Jim added, nodding to Mary.

<u>II</u>

One week earlier…

It was dusk. Jim turned on the headlights of the sand colored Land Rover that sped along the pavement. Six lay in the back seat with his head resting in Mary's lap who had been asleep for nearly four hours. Jim swerved slightly to dodge a shredded tire. Mary's head bobbed forward and her eyes opened.

"Good, you're awake." Jim grinned, making eye contact with her in the rearview mirror.

"You uh," Mary yawned, "need me to drive again?"

"No I'm good. I just thought you'd want to check out the sky. I've never seen it this purple. Not since before…" Mary rolled down the window and felt the wind brush her face.

"Hmm. It's beautiful," she said, as Six lifted his head to yawn. Mary's eyes widened. "What the fuck? We're on a bridge?! Where are we?"

"Just past Key West, on the old Seven Mile Bridge. I've been to Miami once before, but after it all happened. This is the easiest way; the cliffs are too hard to scale with the supplies we have. Not unless we cut through Hell's heart and tried NOLA, but who wants to do that?"

"Hmm, right." Mary yawned. "Does anyone run it?

"Run it?"

"The bridge. Back in Cuba, everything was run by someone. There isn't anything that's free anymore." Mary rubbed Six's face as she spoke. He licked her hands and then buried his nose in her stomach.

"Except the Badlands." Jim stared straight ahead as he spoke. Large rolling and winding dunes spread to the horizon. Each was dark with a slight purple glow at their peaks. Birds circled the air over some of them. Vultures. Some drifters never make it.

"What the shit?" Jim mumbled as he pressed on the brakes. The bridge turned and about eight cars came into view, all stopped. Some were running, others were off with their doors open. Some people, men and women, stood staring straight ahead. Jim braked and shut off the SUV about fifty yards back from the group. Mary leaned forward between the two front seats.

"What do ya think Hellion?" Jim smirked.

"You're seriously still calling me that? I thought me punching you in the gut meant for you to stop."

"Well you are a troublemaker." Jim paused and locked eyes with Mary who glared at him. "Sorry, I couldn't help it."

"It's fine, Fiend."

"Fuck you," said Jim smiling.

"Fuck you too," Mary smiled back, rubbing his shoulder. "Let's go check it out. Six, stay." Six cocked his head letting out a slight whimper and then curled up in the back seat.

Mary walked through the center of the bridge between parked cars while Jim cut around the side. She held her AK out in front of her, walking carefully toward a now gathered crowd. A mother nursing a young baby stared up at Mary and simply shook her head. Mary stopped a moment, forcefully racked a round into the chamber, and strode forward.

"You can't do that!" One tall, thin man shouted. A chorus of shouts erupted as men and women pleaded and exclaimed chaotic words. "We don't have anymore medicine to give you—why would we have any weapons—we just need to get to the city—Please don't—what is this? —I'll sleep with you, that's all I can offer—no you can't!" Everyone suddenly turned at the sound of a sharp whistle.

"What the fuck is going on?!" shouted Jim, who had snuck behind several of the cars and now found himself standing at the front of the crowd. Mary peered through people to see the adversaries. Five men stood in front of three armored pickup trucks which blocked the bridge. They wore tattered, shredded clothing made of some kind of dark material and donned leather motorcycle jackets with silver studs. Each held an automatic weapon and had black and red paint in different designs on their faces and shaved heads.

"No weapons allowed mate! This is our bridge. You pay the toll to the King Troll or you go." The man in the center had spoken, stepping forward.

"Stand down." Jim spoke calmly. "We don't have to kill you…but we sure as hell won't hesitate. Just move and we can all be on our way." The five trolls erupted in laughter.

"This fucker for real?" one asked. "Fuck this Hell Face lets lead-dead 'em."

"Hey boys." Mary grinned as she spoke. Jim grinned at well at her cleverness—she had managed to sneak behind them while he was talking. She always knew how to use her surroundings. The trolls began to quickly shuffle their feet to turn. "Don't *FUCKING* turn around! My friend already warned you that we don't hesitate. You have three seconds to drop your weapons, get in your trucks, and leave." A young girl in the crowd looked past the troll, making eye contact with Mary. Her face relaxed and her concerned eyebrows lowered. Mary pressed the muzzle of her rifle into the back of the neck of one of the trolls. "*NOW!*"

"Shit Grodo…you told me these was easy pickins, no lead weapons here," the troll on the end said.

"Fuck you Donno, I ain't usually misinformed. Drop'em mates, King Troll will deal with these Hell Faces later." The five trolls dropped their weapons and ran past Mary towards their trucks.

"Wait." Mary grabbed one by the collar. "Your name isn't Madonna. Take the jacket off." The troll slid his arms out without turning to face her. The trucks hummed as the engines started and each one sped away toward the city.

"Cowards," Mary said winking toward Jim. Mary turned from him and met the crowd. Each stared at her blankly. Every mouth was open.

"Th-thank you," said the young girl. "Anytime kid." Mary winked at her as she spoke. The crowd went back to their cars as Jim walked over towards Mary.

"So we're Hell Faces huh?" Jim said, nudging her in the arm.

"You and me both." Mary sighed. "Jim?"

"Yeah?"

"These people, they didn't have any way to defend themselves. I mean I know we're tough, but even these people could've stood up to those jokers if they had weapons."

"And we have 15 spare AKs in the back of the truck is what you're saying." Jim raised his eyebrow.

"There's just the two of us. An armed group like these people, *normal* people, that only helps us too. Besides," Mary said, turning, "I'm diggin' those MPXs the trolls left behind."

<u>III</u>

"Are you fuckin serious?" Saint Mako raised his brows and squinted his eyes often when he asked a question, as if to say *fuck you, prove it* to every one who dared bring him bad news. He was a tall, muscular man with pale tattooed skin, a wiry red beard, and a long red braided Mohawk that hung off the back of his head, always resting on his leather vest. He leaned back into the purple leather couch and took a gulp of his Corona. Seven of his men stood behind him. Each one wore leather and had tattoos covering their arms. Some had shaved heads, others had mohawks. All had Glocks.

53

"Dead serious boss. Some small bitch and some kinda Rambo lookin ass hole took our stuff and made us leave the bridge man." One of the trolls shivered a little as he spoke. The other troll just stood silently behind him. Two dancing girls in thongs and heels walked over towards the couch.

"Any more drinks Mako baby?" One of them said as she popped her gum.

"I'm having a *FUCKING MEETING!*" Mako screamed, hurling the bottle at Jessica. It hit her in the jaw and then shattered when it hit the floor. Beer dripped off of her skin and hair. The men behind Mako laughed; one of them walked over to Jessica and gave her a towel, only to squeeze her ass. The men continued to snicker. Carlotta put her arms around Jessica as the two hurried towards the back of the club, their skin changing colors from yellow to pink to blue with every new flash of neon light.

"As I was saying," Mako continued. "You let some ass hole and some small bitch take all FIVE of your MPX's?"

"Daddy says no, daddy says no." Mako quickly turned and saw Charlotte laying across one of the couches, coloring on one of the menus. She was sixteen, with black wavy hair and overalls. She wore headphones over her ears to block the noise and always held tightly onto "Monkey" her small stuffed pink toy.

"Goddammit Mikey!" Mako spat. "Why did you bring your fucking retard niece here to MY fucking strip club?"

"She ain't doing nothing." Mikey shrugged his shoulders as he took out a cigarette.

"Get her out of here now, or I'll shoot your balls with a shark bite."

Mikey quickly turned and took Charlotte's hand and led her out of the back.

"You're lucky she MADE THE CUT! Fifteen and younger are getting rounded up ya know." Mako yelled as Mikey and his niece disappeared through the back door.

"Saint Mako, sir." One of the trolls swallowed before continuing to speak. "What is a shark bite?"

"I'm glad you asked," Mako said as he stood and unholstered his pistol shooting the troll in the chest. Then he shot the other one. Nothing happened. "See that small blinking metal bead stuck to each of your shirts? Those are shark bites. You have about, ohh seven seconds before they explode." As Mako finished talking two of his men grabbed each of the trolls by their hair and slung them back, as they slid across the floor. "You fucked up men, Adios!"

"Wai…" ***BOOMMM!!!*** The troll barely got the word out when it happened. The floor and couch and walls and most of the men were instantly covered with blood and skin and pieces of gut and cloth. Mako turned back to his men, smiling, as he wiped some blood from his chin.

"Have the shitheads clean this up. And Rocco, find this ass hole and the little bitch."

<u>IV</u>

"Madonna, huh." Jim smirked as he looked at the back of Mary's new jacket. It was now night. A few of the cars were still camped on the bridge just ahead of their Land Rover. A light wind washed over the purple and black dunes underneath the light blue glow of the moon.

"No one claimed it," she shrugged. She turned her neck to look in the car's side mirror. The letters were spelled out like a name on the back of a jersey in shiny silver studs.

"Well, it does fit, and you are kind of a Madonna." Jim laughed, leaning against the back bumper as he checked the magazine well of his AK.

"You motherfucker!" Mary punched his arm. "Are you saying I'm vain!"

"Of course not, then you'd be a *primadonna*. I only meant that you are kinda like, well you know." Mary just stared at him. "Did you ever go to Sunday School?" He continued. Her eyes widened.

"So I'm like the Virgin Mary? *HA!*"

"Well you *are* pregnant…in an unusual way." Jim lightly punched her back.

"Well, if this is the Nativity story…we need to get to a fuckin' Bethlehem and fast. And there better be three dudes with gifts…like some red dot sights for these." Mary grinned, resting her hands on her two new MPXs strapped into leg holsters.

56

"Ha, right. That sounds good to me." Jim said as he opened the back door and sat in the seat. Six was curled up and sleeping in the back cargo area. "You want first watch tonight or should I take it?"

"I got it, get some sleep." Just as Mary finished speaking, a young man and his wife approached. She had one of the AKs that Mary had given out slung on her shoulder.

"Miss," the wife began. "We wanted to thank you." Mary turned and Jim sat up.

"Of course," Mary began. "They were given to help us, so we figured we'd return the favor and you guys could use 'em."

"My name is Jane; this is my husband Rolando. These are for you." Jane held out a black shirt and a grey sweatshirt. "It's not much, but we have plenty of clothing. The shirt looks like it would fit you, the sweatshirt for him." She smiled.

"Thank you." Mary said, forcing a smile.

"Have you ever been out there? In Hell?" Rolando interjected. He quivered a bit as he spoke. "Without a gun. Without anything?" His eyes grew glossy.

"Yes." Jim said. "I have. It's like being—

"Trapped. Like no matter where you go, you're in someone's cage." The man said. Jim nodded. "This is what you have done," he said, nodding to his wife and the rifle. "You've opened the cage for us."

"Take care of each other." Jim sighed. "That's the only way on this helluv an earth."

<u>V</u>

The next morning, the Land Rover continued its journey across the bridge above Hell. It was early and the sky began to glow a dark blue. Jim was sleeping in the back and Six had crawled over the seat to sleep on his legs. Mary glanced out the window and saw two lights below, several miles to the west. *Pirates*, she thought, frowning. Suddenly tall buildings appeared in the distance. Jim had sat up and rubbed Mary's shoulder.

"Hey, this is it. Better let me drive."

"Why?"

"Cause," Jim rubbed his eyes. "Last time I was here, the people in charge were pretty chauvinistic." He grinned, "Besides, everyone knows women can't drive!"

"It's too early for jokes asshole!" Mary grinned. "Fine, come on up."

"Miami." Jim said under his breath, taking the wheel. Six yawned and perked up his ears and stuck his head out of the back right window. Mary began inspecting the sights on her new guns.

"What the hell is that?" Mary asked as she nodded ahead at a large metal gateway at the end of the bridge. The city stood beyond it, across the sand and against the now pink sky and orange sun. Most of the buildings were in tact except for some of the larger ones—the tops had crumbled. Dried palm trees were still present along the winding highway which ran next to Old South Beach and purple, green, pink, and yellow neon lights in building windows electrified the city with a colorful haze.

"More trouble? Make sure you're locked and loaded like I know you are." Jim sighed. The gates squealed open with a loud metallic clang and a large beefy man with leather chaps and vest, but no shirt, and covered in tattoos approached Jim's side of the car who cracked open the window.

"Hi." Jim said quickly, clenching his teeth behind a fake smirk.

"Morning." The man responded in a deep voice. "This is the Saint's turf as yer know. Obey the rules, mind your own business, and everything will go well for you."

"Of course." Jim flashed his teeth. "We're good at all that." The man stepped back and waved them through and onto Beach Alley, the main highway around the city.

"As we know? Who's the saint?" asked Mary.

"Not a clue." Jim said, staring at the man in the rearview mirror as he turned onto the highway.

The Land Rover raced down Beach Alley and into the city. Several old snow mobiles and ATV's, covered in sand and loaded with supplies were parked along the road. "Pirate Traders," Jim said. Six sat up and cocked his head to the side, starring out the window at the buildings and the people as Jim slowed, approaching heart of the city. *I didn't expect this many* people, thought Mary. Most of the men wore grey or navy jumpsuits or very old jeans and shirts. Most of the women wore pink, blue, or yellow string bikinis. *Chauvinist is right, fuck!* Mary thought. Everyone else wore dark leather pants, vest, jackets and had some kind of punk rock hair. They were the ones with the guns. A blue Corvette, followed by five black motorcycles roared through the intersection going the opposite direction. The few cars had pulled over to let them through. The women in bikinis who were on the sidewalks all gave a slight bow as the caravan sped through.

"And that's the one who runs it," Mary said, turning her head as the car and bikes tore through the street. Six barked at them through the window.

"Yeah." Jim nodded, looking in the rearview mirror. "I bet you're right."

"Of course I am," Mary smirked.

"We shouldn't stay out in the open long," said Jim as he surveyed the sidewalks through the windows.

"Yeah, let's find a place to lay low," Mary replied, reaching back to rub Six's head. Jim then saw a young girl crossing the street. She was maybe in her teens, but dressed much younger. She had black wavy hair, had on large headphones, and carried a pink stuffed monkey. She briefly made eye contact with him before being yanked on her arm by the large, bearded, leather-clad man she was with. Jim stared at her a moment longer and then turned down a side street and drove to the back side of town. A man in a navy jumpsuit was sweeping the alley. Mary rolled down her window.

"Hey, is there any place to—

"Oh please give me more time! I thought you weren't coming until tomorrow!" the man shuddered and bowed his head.

"What?"

"The Saint's inspection, I thought it was tomorrow."

"Look I don't know who the fuck this Saint person is but we're just looking for a place to stay." The man slowly raised his head. He had short blonde-grey hair and blue eyes.

"Y-you're not from here. Your hell faces!" He almost whispered.

"Yeah that's the second time we've heard that today. Look, we don't know the town and we just need to rest." Mary sighed. The man was silent for a moment; he noticed Mary's face tattoo.

"You can stay with me and the other servants. Follow me." The man began walking down the alley and off onto the sand.

"Why not." Jim said with a shrug, nudging Mary.

<u>**VI**</u>

Jim parked their SUV behind a sand dune just off the road and he, Mary, and Six all followed the man to the edge of the cliff.

"Where the hell do you live?" asked Mary.

"In the cliff. They can't bother them down there." The man reached a wooden ladder that was fastened to the cliff edge with steel pegs and rope. He threw his leg over and began to climb down.

"Who's them?" Mary asked.

"The children."

Mary went second down the ladder followed by Jim who had hoisted Six onto his shoulders. They descended about twenty feet and then reached a rather wide ledge. There was a smallish opening in the side of the rock. The man turned to them before entering.

"My name's Fargo. This is what we call underground Miami." Mary flicked on the light of one of her MPXs and Jim slung his AK over his shoulder and unholstered his HK, equipped with a light. They followed Fargo through an initially narrow passage that widened rather quickly. A soft roar could be heard echoing through the passage. Reaching the opening, Mary gasped. A large cavern loomed before them. The air was cool and the rock walls sparkled and shimmered with bits of quartz and splashing water. The roaring water—a large waterfall poured from the

———

top of one of the rock faces and into a pool below. Several lights had been fastened to the walls creating clear pathways. There were nearly thirty tents and huts set up along the floor of the cavern by the edge of the pool. There were families. Mary had almost forgotten what they looked like. Women carried newborns and toddlers. Men held the hands of their little boys and girls. Everyone wore dirty, tattered clothing, yet it was normal.

"Everyone!" Fargo shouted. Nearly sixty people froze and looked up at the top of the path. "I have brought two visitors. They are good people; welcome them!"

"Why do you trust us?" Jim whispered to Fargo.

"The same reason you apparently trust me. I haven't tried anything yet, and you don't have many options." Fargo smiled. "Ya know the shark gang have itchy trigger fingers and I'm assuming you've run into similar people. You haven't shot me yet. It's the person behind the gun that matters, right?" Fargo patted Jim's shoulder and smiled at Mary. Six panted and yawned.

Mary, Jim, and Six followed Fargo down the rocky path and to the floor of the cavern. Several young girls ran up and grabbed Mary's legs, giggling. Jim smiled.

"And what are your names?" Mary asked, squatting down. Six nudged one of the girls with his head and licked her cheek.

"I'm Sara," said one with black hair.

"Nico," said another.

"Virginia!" giggled the girl who was being licked to death by Six.

"I'm Mary," she smiled, "that's Six. And this is my—Jim." Mary looked back up at Jim who was still standing a few feet back, smiling. "He's my best friend," she said, staring at him.

"Excuse me, sir," a man with dark curly hair ran up to Jim. "Fargo, do you think this man could help? Could they help?!" turning back to Jim, "Sir, my name is Marcos. My wife, and Fargo's wife too, they were—they were captured several months ago. They were made to dance." The man's eyes began to glaze and his lips trembled.

"Dance?" Mary stood as she spoke and walked over towards the men.

"The Saint, Mako, he runs the town. Everything must be as he sees fit, those are the orders. I suppose he found my wife, and Fargo's—attractive. They were forced to dance at his club or be killed. He would kill our children if he knew we had any."

"How does he not—know?" Jim asked when Mary grabbed his arm.

"Look." She said. "I've never seen so many children in one place. They're all down here." Mary sighed.

"We've tried several times to break them free," Fargo interjected. "There's too many of them up there and we don't have any weapons.

"Let me guess," said Mary. "He drives the Blue Corvette Stingray." Fargo nodded.

"Where is this club?" Jim asked.

"It's in uptown, near the Castle."

"Castle?" Mary asked.

"The Castle," Fargo began, "used to be a kind of a prison, for legit crime. That was before Mako took over. It provided some kind of law and order. We suspect it's where they've taken the children, the unlucky ones who aren't down here."

"What the fuck?" Jim huffed.

"Saint Mako, he gets his orders higher up. We're not sure where." Fargo said.

"But I overheard some of his men talking," Marcos began, "when I was cleaning Mako's place. Every person fifteen and under is supposed to be processed."

"Killed," said Mary, touching her tattoo under her right eye. "When I was younger, living in Cuba, a similar order was given. We each got a tattoo marking us. I was fifteen." Jim glanced at Mary's cheek and then down at the floor of the cave.

"How the hell did you two get through the gate without being registered?" Marcos asked.

"Look at them," Fargo cut in, "they look like them." Mary looked over at Jim's weapons and tattoos covering his lower arm. Jim glanced at Mary's leather jacket.

"Their mistake," said Mary.

VII

It was cool in the cavern, especially at night. Jim had brought down the remaining two AKs and a few pistols from the SUV and given them to Fargo and Marcos. He lay at the opening of the cavern and closed his eyes, darkening the shimmering stars against the deep blue sky from his view. Jim felt someone shake his shoulder. Then again. He peeled his eyes open.

"Mary?" He groaned. "Wh—wait, the fuck?!" Jim pulled back and sat up quickly. A girl stood just in front of him. She had dark hair and held onto a pink stuffed gorilla. She looked about fifteen or sixteen, but seemed so much younger. "Who are you?!"

"Are you, are you, are you," she said.

"The fuck?"

"The fuck, the fuck, the fuck."

"Wait…" Jim sighed. *I saw you.*

"Charlotte!" She waved.

"Jim." He said, nodding his head.

"Visit?!" she exclaimed, sitting down cross legged.

"Uh, sure." Jim looked back through the opening hoping Mary would come up to see his new friend. "Look, wait here." Jim stood and motioned with his hand for her to stay seated. Halfway down the passage he met Mary and Fargo. "Mary, you need to follow me, quick. You too." Jim nodded.

"I know her." Fargo said when they reached the opening. Charlotte was still sitting, playing with her gorilla. "She's related to one of Mako's men. She sneaks away sometimes to visit the other children here. She's never given us away, and I haven't had the heart to turn her away, but she can't stay either."

"She has autism, doesn't she?" Jim asked.

"I think so, or something. She's very open to children and to men, probably because those are the only two groups she really sees. Mako and his men have left her alone for the most part, but the processing is coming, and I don't know where she'll end up. She's old enough to make the cut, but disability isn't something that's tolerated here."

"My sister had autism. Before…" Jim paused. Mary reached for his hand, then stopped.

"Books?!" Charlotte beamed up at Jim.

"I'll go get you something for you to read to her," smiled Fargo.

"Wait—I." Jim paused. "Sure." Jim leaned against the rock wall and slid down to sit. Charlotte stood and walked over and sat next to him. Mary bit her lower lip to keep from laughing. Jim shook his head, then smiled.

"Friends?!" Charlotte asked.

"Yeah, friends." Jim smiled. He glanced up at Mary.

"You know," Mary began, "this is good."

"What is?"

"Seeing the other side of the world. There are still good people."

Jim read to Charlotte for nearly two hours from Jane Austen's *Sense and Sensibility*. Mary had brought Jim's sweatshirt back up as the night grew colder; Charlotte ended up using it as a blanket and eventually fell asleep.

"Some kinda shit we walked into huh?" Mary let out a quick laugh and then frowned.

"You think we should help." Jim said.

"I mean—

"I wasn't asking if you think it; I can see it. You want to help." Jim sighed. Mary nodded her head in reply.

"I just wanted to escape part of the world. But something in me won't let me just go and forget. What if North Dakota isn't even real or not the real that I'm expecting." Mary wrapped her arms around her stomach.

"Well I'm here for you. No matter what." Jim smiled.

"Why the hell did we get stuck together?" Mary's eye brows raised.

"Destiny?" Jim smirked, "Or maybe I have that same feeling that won't let me just go and forget. We had to meet. To do what we do best. Let's stay. Let's help." Mary smiled and briefly closed her eyes. For a brief moment she saw the ocean. Blue water splashing on her mom and her dad as she sat in the sand. Heaven.

"Thanks," she said. "There's no one I'd rather fuck up bad guys with." She laughed softly, tying not to wake Charlotte.

"Fuck I could use a drink right now, but…" Mary touched her stomach. Jim smiled.

"Met too."

"Goodnight."

"Night Mary." Jim closed his eyes.

The sun peaked over the pink and blue sand dunes below—down in Hell. Jim stretched his neck to one side, then opened his eyes. Charlotte, the book, and his sweatshirt were gone. Six ran up and barked, then licked his face.

"Ok, I'm up, I'm up." Jim wiped his face and then rubbed Six's head as he made his way down to the cavern. There was a small fire burning in a stone circle by the pool. Some of the men and women had made breakfast.

"Here, do you drink coffee?" one of the women asked.

"Yes, yes I do." Jim grinned. "Thank you, mam." Jim went and sat next to Mary.

"Morning," Jim said, nodding to everyone. Fargo and Marcos sat by an elderly couple. A few of the children ran over to pet Six who had followed Jim down.

"So finish telling me, how did Mako take control?" Mary asked the elderly black man sitting across the fire.

"It was about two years ago. Miami was one of the few cities on the edge of Hell that hadn't fallen yet. Three elders led the city in truth and fairness. Everyone was respectful. Everyone was armed. Everyone was free. Mako and his men broke through our gate with a horde of Darkfaces. He executed the three elders in the heart of the city, decapitating them and saying, *I'm in charge now.* He threw their heads onto the street in the midst of a crowd of women and children. The Darkfaces took our guns. Some resisted. They were killed too." The man's lips quivered a bit. He paused, took a sip of coffee, and then continued. "Other cities are the same. Ruled by one who submits to a far off authority, but each is allowed to rule how they see fit. Here they kill gay people, and lesbians, and transgendered people, all because Mako despises them. In the Tampa Bay Fortress, they kill heterosexuals because *their* leader despises them. The Darkfaces—they somehow support— sponsor all of this. It is their will that all leaders have all authority to do whatever they want."

"Might makes right," Jim said.

"Exactly," the man whispered. "Exactly."

"What about the children?" Mary asked after taking a sip of coffee. She looked over at the young girls playing with Six. "What do the Darkfaces want with them?"

"Death," whispered the man. "Years ago, when I could still travel," he smiled and nudged the elderly woman beside him, "I was in Mexico—it fell first to the Darkface Lord. In their pride they declared that they would be the last generation of this dying earth."

"No kids, then nothing can come after." Jim said to himself as he stared down at two slices of bacon. Mary looked over at him and touched his knee, smiling. *We're gonna stop this*, she thought.

"Tomorrow." Jim said. Everyone looked up. "We should shut it all down tomorrow." Mary nodded.

"Yeah," she said. "We can. I'll start coming up with some plans. Maybe it'll include chopping off Mako's head." Mary took one last swig of coffee and stood up to walk back towards one of the tents.

"Where did you find her?" the elderly man asked with a soft chuckle.

"Killing Darkfaces in Havana." Jim shrugged. "So yeah, she's the most dangerous person in the city."

Later that day Jim sat by the opening of the cavern, just as he had with Charlotte the night before. Six lay beside him as he cleaned his rifle and stared out across Hell.

"Jim?" Mary appeared and walked over to sit by him. "You ok?"

"Yeah." Jim looked at her. She raised her eyebrows. *She knows I'm lying.* "Look, I guess I just was trying to decide if I keep finding myself in the wrong place at the wrong time…or the right time." Mary sat down beside him.

"I know you found me at the right time." She said, nudging him. "I wouldn't be here. Captain Hyde's daughter, Elizabeth wouldn't be here. Maybe—

"Maybe what?"

"Maybe, this is what I'm supposed to do. What—we're supposed to do. Not just now, for these people. But maybe all the time." Jim starred at her eyes, then her lips, then her eyes again.

"How's the baby doing?" he asked, looking back down at his gun.

"So far so good." Mary smiled. Suddenly Six barked. Some kind of grey fabric fell from the edge of the cliff and landed just in front of Jim's feet. Mary went to pick it up, then looked up.

"What is it?" asked Jim.

"Well, I don't know if she's sticking around, but I think you have a new best friend." Mary smiled, and held up Jim's sweatshirt. A blue and yellow fabric puzzle piece had been sewn onto the chest. Mary winked at Jim.

The morning came quickly; Jim ate while he checked his AK and his HK .45. Mary walked over to Nico and a few of the other children.

"Six is going to stay here while we're out today. Take care of him," Mary rubbed Six's head. "He's my very special friend. Stay." Mary motioned to Six as she winked at Nico and the others.

"Hey, Jim," Fargo walked over with his AK slung over his back. "Look I know you know what you're doing. But watch out for these." He held out his hand and on it was a small, metallic looking clamp.

"What is it?"

"Well this one's inactive, but it's a small explosive. Mako loads them into his .45. They clamp onto you and detonate in a few seconds. He calls them sharkbites, the asshole." Fargo put it back in his pocket and his right hand started to shake.

"Look," Jim began, "Thanks. You'll be fine. We're gonna get her back. All of them. I promise."

"So what's the plan?" Marcos asked anxiously.

"She's the mastermind." Jim nodded to Mary.

"Yeah. I have an idea. We can save your wives *and* the kids. Today." She paused. "And give you back Miami."

<u>**IX**</u>

Most of the neon lights of the Shark Attack club were dead. The few that hadn't been shot to hell buzzed and flickered.

"Y-you b-bit-tch!" The man with the green mohawk coughed blood as he spoke. ***Crack!!!*** Blood and flesh sprayed the carpet and walls after Mary pulled the trigger. .50 caliber rounds will do that to a person's head.

An elderly man stood up from behind a counter with his hands up. He wore a white collared short-sleeve shirt. He shivered.

"Do you realize what you've d-d-done?!" He exclaimed, but almost as a whisper. "This is Saint Mako's club…He w-won't like it."

"We know," Mary sighed. "We'll fuck him up too."

"What she said." Jim added, nodding to Mary.

Jim ran out the back to start up the Land Rover. Fargo and Marcos each walked out with their wives—Mary had given her jacket to Carlotta and her Metallica shirt to Victoria. Mary's new Nirvana shirt fit perfectly as she slid it on before going out.

"Lay low," Mary said to the rest of the dancers who had congregated in the main stage area. "Shit's going down. Mako is done. Take whatever Shark gang guns are on the floor." Mary handed one of her MPXs to the oldest woman. "There's a full mag in there. Just keep the safety off; this is your safety." Mary motioned with her index finger and winked. Mary turned to run out the back door.

"Hey, what's your name?" one of the girls asked.

"Mary, why don't you fill them in on the plan," Jim said, speeding back towards the edge of the cavern.

"Victoria, right?" Victoria nodded towards Mary as Fargo caressed her cheek. Marcos and this man Jim are going to take you and Carlotta back to the underground. Fargo and I have to go start the next phase of the plan." Victoria wiped tears and mascara from her eyes.

"What is that?"

"Saving Miami." Mary said, smiling.

"And then Jim and I have to meet up with them, but you will be safe in the underground until we get back," Marcos said, holding Carlotta in his arms.

"Don't leave me baby, please." Carlotta squeezes his arms and pressed her head into his neck.

"We won't be long. We have to save the children. We'll make it through this *mi Amor.*"

"Remember, we meet at Mako's mansion, the Reef, after it goes off," Jim said, looking at Mary in the rearview mirror. Mary checked the magazine in her new Desert Eagle. Two rounds. She racked the slide and then rested her arm on her stomach. *We're saving the children,* she thought.

"Um, Sir?" Mako threw the naked dark girl off of him and wrapped a towel around his waist.

"I'm kinda in the middle of something Rocco. What?!" The girl wrapped one of the sheets around her and quickly ran into the bathroom, shutting the door.

"Um, the children. And the, the dancers. Are…gone." Mako clenched his teeth and strode over toward his desk, grabbing his gun belt.

"Go get in the truck, and find my keys."

"Also, the flatbed and your Corvette have been…stolen."

"Open your mouth."

"Wh-what?"

"*Open*…your mouth." Rocco quivered. "I liked you." Mako said as he drew his pistol and thrust the muzzle into Rocco's mouth. "But this shit can't slide. This is a sharkbite. It's gonna fuckin' suck. But please, *PLEASE*, try. For the first time, to take it like a man." Rocco's face went pale. He began to sweat. Mako slowly pulled the barrel out of Rocco's mouth. "Or, *GO GET MY FUCKING SHIT BACK!*"

"*FUCK!* This thing is fast!" Mary said to herself, shifting gears in the Blue Corvette. "Hey Marcos, how're the kids doin'?" Mary spoke into the walkie clipped to her shirt.

"So far so good." Marcos's words were somewhat muffled in the speaker.

"If the border Sharks or Trolls try and stop us, it'll be on Beach Alley. Stay sharp," Fargo interjected.

"You too." Mary shifted gears again and sped past the covered flatbed and down the street, weaving in and out of a few cars, which pulled over at the sight of the blue and silver car. *Fuckers think I'm Mako driving this thing. No idea how much he controlled this city.* The Vette followed by the truck turned onto beach ally. It was dusk. Neon lights from all of Mako's clubs flickered on. This was *his* Miami. *For now,* Mary thought. Mary shifted down with the paddle shifters.

"Mary." Fargo radioed in

"Talk to me."

"This is it. I hope your plan works." Mary slowed and turned off onto a service road. The truck sped on and approached gate one. A semi truck, a Dodge Challenger, and seven BMW motorcycles blocked the gateway. The engines revved and the headlights flicked on as Fargo's truck braked.

"Step out of the truck Fargo." Mako spoke through a megaphone. "Those kids and those bitches are *mine*. Walk away and y.."

PROUUMMMMMmmmmMMMMmmmmmMMMmmmMM!! Mary had sped off of the service road and braked hard, stopping perpendicular to the truck and right in front of Mako's Challenger. Mako's eyes widened. The Corvette's engine purred.

"Hope you don't mind; I borrowed your ride." Mary spat, holding up her middle finger. She shifted gears and the back tires spun violent smoke as the rear of the car turned and knocked down two of the motorcycles. The Corvette sped back down Beach Alley as Mako's Challenger followed.

Fargo slammed on the gas with his foot and the flatbed truck rammed into one of the trucks blocking the gate entrance. Two of Mako's men on the motorcycles sped off to follow their master while the others dismounted and approached the truck with their M4s.

"Get out of the truck you dumb fuck!" Rocco yelled at Fargo as he and the other men surrounded the truck. He did as he said and put his hands behind his head, stepping out of the truck and following Rocco around the back to open the door.

"These children," Rocco snickered as Fargo began to open the door. "They are so screwed now. Thanks to *you*."

"Now." Fargo had whispered into his jacket collar.

"*Now?*" said Rocco. "Now, *what?*" Fargo pushed past a few of the men and dove toward a ditch before the men could react.

BBBOOOOOOOMMMMMMM!!!

Vrrrrooumnmmmmmmm!! Mary sped down the highway, violently shifting gears. Mako kept pace as his Challenger stayed present in the rear view mirror. The racing cars weaved through pirate traders and a few of the other cars from the city, creating a violent blur of color. The blue Corvette and the Purple Challenger gleamed in the half sunken orange sun as the fading light shone across the water and onto the neon city beneath the neon pink sky.

Suddenly, the two motorcycles entered the highway from an on ramp and flanked Mary's Vette. Mako's Challenger slowed and exited. *What the f-* Mary thought. The two bikes and their black clad riders continued to shift gears and sped along on either side of the Corvette. Each of the drivers pulled an Uzi from their sides and aimed at Mary's windows. Mary glanced in her side mirrors, then braked hard. The motorcycles shot forward as the Corvette tires squealed and burned, bringing the car to an immediate halt. One of the motorcycles had turned to find the Corvette when **SHINGHHG!** The riders head was severed instantly by a low road sign. The bike lost control and slid across the road with the body still gripping the seat. The head remained in the helmet and rolled and bounced across several lanes, spurting red every rotation it made. The second motorcycle braked hard and slid around to look back toward Mary. The Corvette crept forward as the driver's side window rolled down. Mary stuck her arm out and grabbed the severed head and threw it in the passenger seat. Blood pooled across the white leather. Mary nodded towards the other motorcycle and then she sped off of the highway and into the heart of the city with the BMW bike close behind.

"Are you INSANE?!" screamed Rocco. Fargo coughed as he stood, covered in sand and dirt. All of the men lay dead on the pavement. Blood was splattered along the road and the sand and Rocco's clothes. "You killed a bunch of kids just to kill us?!"

"Look again shithead!" Fargo sneered. Rocco turned to look through the flames and the smoke. There were no charred bodies, only bits of paper and straw. Rocco turned sharply to face Fargo who had picked up one of the guns and pointed it at Rocco's face.

"Please, just—

CRACK! CRACK! CRACK! CRACK! CRACK! CRACK!

Fargo sighed as the body fell to the ground, chest and face torn open. He then began to walk down Beach Alley, then jog, towards the Reef.

The Reef was a large white brick mansion surrounded by palm trees and a courtyard of sculptures taken from abandoned places from before. There were usually lights along the driveway. They had been shot out.

"Where's Charlotte?!" Jim spat. He punched the guard in the face again. The rest of the small guard unit lay dead in the courtyard. The moon light shimmered in the pools of blood on the stone drive. Jim and Marcos were now covered in that same blood. None of it was their own.

"Maybe she's not here Jim." Marcos said, peeking his head back out into the hallway where thirty small boys and girls sat huddled against the wall. Jim turned to the doorway and glared at him.

"She's here somewhere." Jim huffed. "Fine. You won't talk. You don't get to live." Jim flicked open his karambit blade and ran it across the man's throat.

"Uh, sir?" A small boy came from out of a closet. He was very thin, wearing only a large grey t-shirt. He had black matted hair and dark skin. Jim stood at once, putting his blade back into his belt.

"What's your name kid?" Jim tried to smile.

"Abel."

"Come here Abel. We are not here to hurt you." The boy took several steps forward. "Here, take this." Jim reached in his bag and pulled out some dried bacon.

"Charlotte!!" Abel exclaimed, noticing the puzzle piece sewn on Jim's shirt. He shuffled quickly towards Jim and took the bacon, stuffing it into his mouth.

"Hey, slow down kid, there's plenty! You know the girl who made this?" Abel nodded his head.

"Where is she? Please, I have to find her." Abel finally swallowed.

"There." He pointed out the window. Jim stood and walked over. It was the Castle.

"Why there?"

"Because Mako decided she needed to be processed. She wasn't worth keeping because she couldn't work."

"Well," Jim looked at Marcos, and then at Abel. "I'm gonna go save her and shut all that fuckin' processing down."

"Let me go with—

"No. Marcos, you need to stay here with the kids and wait for Mary." Jim racked the first round into his AK and strode toward the door. He looked back. "I've done shit like this before."

Mary's blue and silver Corvette gleamed in the sinking Miami sun. She squeezed the paddles with her fingers, shifting gears as the black BMW bike sped behind her. Wide open sand dunes disappeared as tall buildings and neon club lights surrounded them as Mary sharply turned down a street leading into the heart of the city. People began looking out of windows and stepping out of doors. Young women, who once shuddered at the sight of Mako's Vette now set their faces with courage towards it, seeing its new driver. Mary glanced over towards the bleeding head, rolling around in the white leather passenger seat. She grinned. The black BMW was dead center in her rearview mirror. Mary braked and turned sharply to the right and crashed through the large glass display windows of an old Saks Fifth Ave. Bits of glass, pearls, diamonds, and cloth shot up over and around the Blue Corvette and sprayed the BMW that fishtailed through the debris before regaining its balance. Mary slowed, the back end of the car swung around, then she accelerated down a wide aisle of clothing and perfume. The lights were on in the store but only a few people were there for a moment before disappearing at the sound of the V8 engine. One female worker in a string bikini (a trademark of a St. Mako employee) hid behind the perfume counter. Mary slowed when she saw her. She braked hard, causing the tires to screech against the marble floor and rock the back end of the car forward, then back again. The engine purred.

"Get in." Mary said as she rolled down the window and nodded towards the back door. The girl quickly jumped in the backseat, carrying a baseball bat. "Can I have that?" The girl nodded towards Mary, handing it to her. The BMW had stopped at the opposite end of the aisle. Its driver throttled the engine and racked a round into his Uzi. The store shimmered in broken glass, jewelry and lights. Mary gripped the bat and held it across her left forearm, just at the edge of the open driver's window. She spun the back end of the car around, spinning smoke, and then accelerated down the aisle. The BMW throttled forward. The two raced violently towards each other. Just as the motorcycle approached, Mary thrust the bat outside the driver's window and turned sharply, knocking the gun from the driver's hand and shattering his helmet with the bat. The BMW slid across the marble floor as the driver crashed into the perfume display, shattering glass everywhere. Mary's Vette braked hard after sliding through several racks of clothing.

The driver's door opened and Mary's black boots were the first thing out of the door. She stood, staring at the crashed BMW for a moment. Clinching her fists, she strode over towards him. He groaned a little but was motionless. Using a shirt that had ripped off of the rack, she carefully picked up a large piece of shattered glass in the shape of a blade. She bent down and pulled the man's helmet off. His face was cut in a thousand places.

"Where's Mako?" Mary spoke through clinched teeth as she pressed the glass to the man's neck.

"I'm—bleeding, out…" the man choked up dark blood and spit it onto the floor. "F-fuck you H-hell Face." Mary stood and dropped the glass. She walked to retrieve the Uzi and pointed it at the floor just to the left of the man's neck.

BaMMMbAMMMBAMBMABAMMMMM!! Each bulled cut through the man's neck until the head was detached from his body. Blood pooled on the marble floor and seeped into the cracks in the tile.

Mary tossed the head next to the other one in the driver's seat. She looked back towards the girl sitting in the back.

"D—does this mean that, that you're in charge now?" Her lip quivered.

"I don't know, but *he* sure as hell isn't." Mary turned back and looked at the windshield. It was covered in clothes. "That can't be comfortable," Mary said, nodding towards her bikini. Reaching out the window Mary tossed back some clothes. "Hope these work. Buckle up kid."

The Corvette sped back through the shattered window, jumping down the curb, and onto the street. There was a large crowd gathered outside the store. Most of the women were just girls, maybe sixteen. They wore the strict dress code of bikinis, or less. The men were in dirt covered jumpsuits or old, tattered clothing. The young girl got out of the Corvette with her new clothes and walked over to the driver's side.

"Thank you. What's your name?"

"Mary." Looking past the girl and toward the crowd she said, "Spread the word." Mary tossed the two heads out of the window. Each bounced once and rolled a few feet across the pavement. As the car sped off through the city, the girl from the store smiled.

<u>X</u>

Two men stood outside of the large double doors at the top of the staircase. The Castle, as the locals called it, sat on the edge of the beach cliff. It was surrounded by tall wood fencing and stood three stories high in light pink brick.

"Jim." Jim reached for the walkie on his AK strap.

"What?" he whispered.

"Abel says the building has thirty men at any given time. The kids are kept on the top floor—that's probably where Charlotte would be."

"Right. Thanks." Jim shut the walkie off. He looked down at the multi-colored puzzle piece embroidered on his grey sweatshirt. He slung his AK over his shoulder and took out his suppressed HK .45.

ZiiipSNAP! ZiiipSNAP! Red splattered the brick behind the two guards' heads as they fell to the ground. Jim holstered his pistol and rushed up the stairs. He unfastened the AK from its sling and quietly opened one of the doors. Three men stood just down the hall and all three looked up towards Jim. *Fuck.*

BudumBAM BAM BAM BbbbbBAMBAM!! Jim shot rounds in burst, hitting all three men. He ran forward, grabbing a grenade from one of their belts as he sprinted past them toward the stairs. *Five down I guess.* Jim ascended the stairs quickly but making every effort to step lightly on his feet. The door at level three opened. Jim glanced up and saw a man with a thick beard and an Uzi look down the stairwell at him. ***ZipPP ZiPCRACK!!!*** The man fired at Jim who dove under one of the stair cases. Looking up, Jim kicked open the door on level two and rolled out into the hall. An alarm siren began to sound. The sound of gun chambers racking and men running filled the large hallway. Jim began jogging, his shadow cast on the floor in spurts every time he passed one of the large windows. He saw a narrow hallway to his right; he turned down it and stopped. A stairway sign was posted on the wall at the end. Before Jim could move, nearly twenty men poured into the hallway from both ends. Everyone was motionless for a moment.

"Evening, fellas." Jim grinned and rolled the grenade toward the men at his back and in a continuous motion raised his AK towards the men in front of him. Jim shot his weapon in bursts, hitting three men who fell to the ground choking on their own blood as lead ripped through their necks. Jim grabbed one of the flailing, bleeding men and briefly hid behind him as the grenade—

KABOOMMMM!!! Bits of drywall, flesh, clothing, and smoke filled and flew through the air. One of the men ran up towards Jim and shoved their pistol into his face. Jim fell onto his back, kicking the man in the knee, causing the bullet to just miss his ear. Jim glared at the man and emptied his AK into his chest. Each bullet ripped through with a rhythmic thud and tear. ***Click, Click.*** *You kidding me?* Jim thought, throwing the rifle at the next two men who lunged through the smoke. Jim dodged one and slammed the other against the wall, taking his suppressed pistol and shooting the man in the face. Jim then turned and kicked the other man, pinning him against the opposite wall and shooting him.

"Drop it, Motherfucker!" shouted a man on the other side of the clearing smoke. Jim turned and shot blindly through the haze and hit someone judging by the thud he heard. ***BBaDUMMMbumBADMUMMM!!!*** The man fired his Uzi at Jim who pressed himself against the wall just as he was hit in the left arm. Jim fired back two rounds and *click*. Empty.

"AGHHH!" Jim lunged at the man, blood streaming down his shoulder. He grabbed the man's neck with his right hand and threw him to the floor.

CRACKKK! The man shot Jim in the stomach with a small pistol he had retrieved from his belt. Jim looked down, wide-eyed and pale. He dropped to his knees. The smoke had cleared and the man stood back up in front of Jim with two other men just behind him.

"I don't know—what the fucking hell you are doing here." The man coughed and rubbed his neck. Jim looked up as blood gushed from his shoulder and side. "But you, you fucked up asshole, really, really bad. The man pressed his pistol into Jim's forehead. *Mary. Charlotte. FUCK YOU.* Jim reached for his karambit and grabbed the man's wrist, pulling it to the floor, who fired twice, breaking up bits of carpet and tile. Jim slashed the man's throat and blood poured out as if it were a faucet. It splattered and pooled on the carpet. He looked at Jim with his eye brows up and mouth open. The two men behind him were frozen. Jim stood, picking up the man's gun. ***CRACK! CRACK!!*** The two men fell to the ground. Jim's right hand shook as he pressed his left arm into his side and limped toward the stairs.

Mary pulled back onto Beach Alley and shifted into fifth gear. The highway curved around the edge of the cliffs of Old South Beach. Pulling her walkie to her mouth Mary said,

"Jim, I lost Mako but the rest of the plan worked. He's probably headed back to the castle to make sure the kids are—

SCREACHHhhhhhCRASHH!!!

Two bright lights had raced toward Mary's side door and the thrust of hundreds of pounds of metal knocked the breath from her chest. The blue Corvette flipped seven times across the highway and onto the rocks and sand at the cliff's edge. Mary opened her eyes slowly. The world was upside down. She unbuckled and fell onto the ceiling of the car and then crawled through the broken windshield. Standing, she felt her head lighten as blood dripped down her cheek.

"I don't know who the *FUCK* you think you are, but this is where I kill you, bitch!" Mary turned and saw Mako standing next to his smoking, crumpled Challenger at the edge of the street.

Jim slowly opened the door on the third floor. Red lights every several yards along the ceiling flashed and the warning siren still blazed through the speakers.

Jim gripped the pistol with both hands. His body switched between grey and red every time the warning light flashed across the large open room with few windows. He hobbled towards a post that ran to the ceiling and fell against it. Jim winced. Looking back, he saw drips and streams of his own blood along the floor. He slid down the pole against his back loosening the grip on the gun until it slid out of his hand.

Suddenly, the Flashing lights and the sirens stopped. Soft footsteps approached him from behind. Jim tried to turn his head but could not.

"You wore it. Wore the puzzle shirt, puzzle shirt, puzzle shirt. Wore it here." A voice said softly. Charlotte walked over to face Jim and knelt by his chest. She pulled up the sweatshirt and tore open a large paper pouch and pressed two thick bandages onto his abdomen and shoulder.

"No more blood, blood blood. No more." She smiled. Jim still lay on his side and reached for the pouch, reading the label.

"Quick-clot wound dressing." Jim raised his eyebrow. "The fuck you know what this is for?"

"Fuck you know, fuck you know, fuck you know." Charlotte replied.

"Ok, don't say that word. Don't say fuck like I do." Jim smiled. "Thanks kid."

"Jim, Jim, Jim, go, go, go, now!" Jim slowly stood as he looked under his shirt. The bleeding stopped *for now*, he thought.

"Ya kid, lets get out of here." Jim coughed, and reached for his radio.

"Marcos, I g—got her."

"Ok but hurry. Mary's not responding on her radio. Just before she went silent she said something about Mako getting away. Fargo said reserve men are falling back to the base. I'll get the children out like we planned."

"Alright kid, lets hustle." Charlotte helped Jim limp back down the stairs and out into the night air.

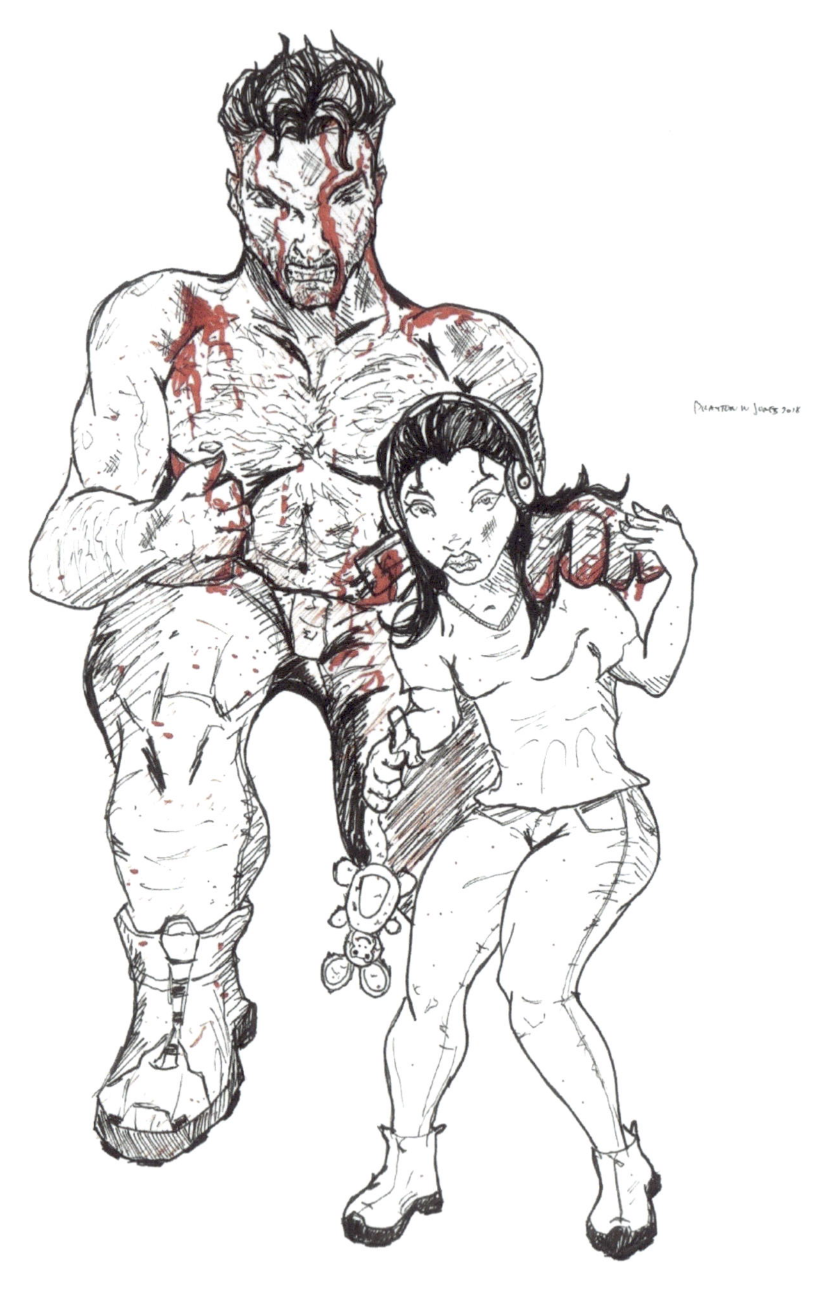

CRACK! CRACK! Mary shot two rounds out of her Desert Eagle as she launched herself backwards over the edge of a small rock bluff and into a pile of sand. Mako shot back violently as .45 bullets tore through the Vette, shattering more glass which rained on Mary as she fell. She summersaulted backwards, and then caught her balance, aiming up at the car sitting on the rock edge. It was dark now. Mary squinted, using the glow from the upside down taillights to scan the rock edge.

Suddenly Mako lunged from around the corner of the rock and punched

Mary square in the eye, then again in the jaw with a left hook. Mary fell back, firing two more shots into the air as blood rushed over her eye.

"You pussy." Make laughed, taking aim at Mary. ***CRACK! CRACK! CRACK!*** Mary rolled quickly down the dune and to the edge of the cliff face that descended into Hell. Each of the bullets zipped into the sand just inches from her.

She slowly stood. Sweat and blood slid down Mary's bruised eye. The wind blew over the edge of the cliff. She gripped the pistol in her hand; she knew it was empty. It started to rain. Water ran over Mary's face and washed the dirt and blood splatter from her face and arms.

"You bitch!" Saint Mako spat dark blood from his mouth onto the dry rocky sand. He extended his arm, aiming his pistol at Mary. "No one's here to save you."

"Just me." Jim limped over from behind one of the large rocks. Shirtless, bleeding, Tomahawk in one hand, HK in the other.

"Shit, you're fucked up bad!" Mako smiled. "Not gonna happen."

CRACK! CRACK! Jim shot two rounds and Mako spun to the side, escaping both. Mako turned quickly and shot Jim in the knee, but nothing happened. Jim looked down and his face went pale. A silver clamp had latched onto his pants. Jim immediately began to rip his pants down—he leapt. ***CRACK-BOOMMM!!!***

"Jim!" Mary screamed. The dust settled. His right leg was gone. Blood began to soak into the sand. Jim's hands shook as he reached for his belt, pulling from his pants, and strapped it around his thigh, tightening it just before passing out.

"He'll bleed out soon." Mako hissed. "Just you and me sweetheart." Mako pressed the muzzle of his pistol into Mary's stomach and began moving his finger toward the trigger.

Rain splashed across Jim's face. He turned his head, grasping for his tomahawk. His fingers fumbled across the handle but he gained a grip. He breathed heavily as he vaulted up on one leg, blood fell like the rain from the other.

"AHHHNOOOOOO!!!!!" Jim roared as he hurled the tomahawk. It spun violently through the rain and wind. *SHUNNKK!* The blade lodged in Mako's shoulder of his shooting arm. Blood spurt and sprayed across Mary's chest and up into Mako's face. His arm and neck convulsed as his finger's loosened their grip on his pistol. Jim had collapsed.

Mako stuttered back towards the cliff, his convulsing fingers grasping for Mary's arm. She gripped the handle on the tomahawk, now digging in and lodging up in his neck. She pulled it in towards her face just for a moment. His eyes widened and his face grew pale.

"Go to hell," she whispered. Mary ripped the handle to the side, tearing Mako's head completely off as the momentum thrust his body backwards over the edge of the cliff. Red colored water descended along side him. Mary barely heard the thud when his body collapsed into the dark sand below. She had just caught his head by the long braided mohawk. Lightning shot across the sky to her back; her silhouette flashed briefly like a painting of David holding the head of Goliath. She quickly turned and rushed back.

"Jim!" Mary dropped the tomahawk and head, sprinting towards Jim. He lay on the sand, motionless. Mary dropped to her knees and held his head in her hands.

"Jim, Jim. Jim please still be here. Jim" She whispered, pressing her ear to his chest. The beating was faint, but there.

"Mary?" Mary quickly looked up and saw Fargo.

"Radio for help! We have to save him!" Mary screamed as tears streamed down her face. "Don't leave," Mary whispered to Jim. "This isn't how this goes.

Don't you die motherfucker."

<u>POST SCENE</u>

"Saint Mako is dead, Medusa, Lord of the Blackfaces." A bearded man with a shaved head and black robes spoke. He held a black and silver helmet down by his waist. The two stood atop a tall cathedral roof in Northern Mexico. The sky was black and most of the stars were covered by clouds.

"And?" Lady Medusa's voice was almost robotic; It was a placid calm. Nothing comforting. She stepped forward as she spoke. She was a very tall and tan skinned woman with a shaved head. She wore a black dress that clung to her in the wind. Golden jewelry clung to her ears, neck, wrists, ankles, and lips. Golden spikes protruded from her head in a single row. All of her adornment could be missed by her distracting pets. Two black cobras, Alpha and Omega, hung from her neck and shoulders, slithering and sliding across her neck and head.

"And," the man swallowed as he momentarily locked eyes with Alpha. "He was killed by the same person who reportedly killed Harrod, one of Captain Hyde's men." Medusa simply raised an eyebrow. The man continued. "She's the so-called bitch from Hell that also killed your blackface ambassadors in Havana."

"Does she have a name?"

THE STORY CONTINUES IN BOOK III

<u>**HELLA FANS**</u>

The people listed below are special. These are the original fans; this group

financially supported *Hell Mary* before it made its way into your hands. Hella Fans,

THANK YOU.

Sarah Abbott
Jesse Acosta
Abby Allison
Michelle Andre
Priscilla Crain
Brent Fischer
Fildaues Hafize
Ashley Hart
Larry Hart
Samantha Hart
Melly Hasenstein
Lexi Henrichs
Kristen Koch
Parker Jennings
Regan Jones
Sandra Lipinoga
Carli Monpetit
Jen Montgomery
Kaitlyn Motschenbacher
Amber Ray
Joel Robertson
Michelle Taylor
Ann Voeltz
Erin VonRuden
James Winkes
Kristy Winkes

Original Art by Jet Falco. Instagram @jetfalco

NIRVANA

NIRVANA

<u>ABOUT THE AUTHOR</u>

Drayton W. Jones resides in the Twin Cities, Minnesota. In addition to writing, he is an illustrator, avid coffee drinker, history enthusiast, and a ferocious movie buff. He made his artist debut at the MCBA MSP ComiCon 2018 as a guest creator. Drayton is pictured below; the picture was taken as a part of a cosplay photo shoot. Drayton's mother wants everyone to know that he does not actually have a tattoo on his neck.

You can follow Drayton on:

Instagram @halfwayhell.productions
Snapchat @draytonw7
Email: draytonwjones7@gmail.com

Photo by Stacey Repinski
www.staceyrepinskiphotography.com